Snow White and the Seven Dwarfs

Once upon a time, there lived a King and Queen who were blessed with a beautiful daughter who was as white as snow. "I will call her Snow White," said the King, joyously. However, the King's happiness was short lived, for the Queen passed away soon after the Princess was born.

1

After some time, the King remarried. The new Queen was extremely proud of her beauty. She even owned a magic mirror. Often she asked it, "Mirror, Mirror, on the wall who's the fairest of them all?"

When the mirror said, "It's you, my Queen." She was content.

Years passed by and Snow White grew up to be far more beautiful and fairer than the Queen. One day, the Queen asked the mirror the same question but the mirror replied,
"You, my Queen, are fair,
But Snow White is fairer still."
The Queen was very shocked and angry to hear this reply. She became jealous of Snow White's beauty.

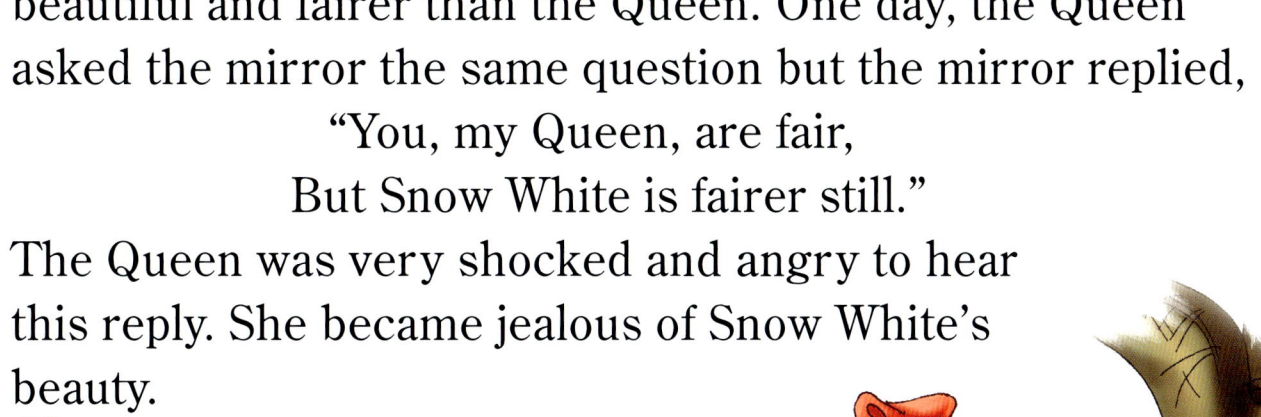

One day, the Queen called a hunter and ordered him, "Take Snow White to the forest and kill her. Remember to bring back her heart as a token of her death." The hunter was shocked when he heard the Queen's command. As it was the Queen's order, he had to take Snow White to the forest.

Once inside the forest, the hunter who was kind and pitiful said to Snow White, "Princess, the Queen has ordered me to kill you but I can't do such a thing." Snow White was very frightened and asked, "What do I do now?" "Run deep into the forest and never show your face to the Queen," replied the hunter.

5

Snow White was very scared and ran deep into the forest. Meanwhile, the hunter killed a rabbit, and took its heart to the Queen. The Queen was pleased to see the heart.

Meanwhile, Snow White walked on and on deep into the forest. She was very tired. After a long time, she saw a little cottage and began walking towards it. She knocked at the door of the cottage but no one answered. After a little thought, she went inside.

Snow White was surprised to see that there was seven tiny chairs at the dining table, seven arm chairs in the drawing room and seven little beds and the cottage was in a terrible mess. She decided to put everything back in order and tidy up the cottage. She cleaned up the whole place and by evening she was exhausted. Snow White lay down on a bed and soon felt asleep.

However, the Dwarfs warned Snow White, "The Queen will soon realise that you are alive. Do not open the door for anyone." Snow White decided that it was safer that way and started living with them.

One day, the Queen asked her mirror again her favourite question. The mirror told her that Snow White, who lived with the dwarfs, was the fairest of all.

The Queen was very angry. Quickly, she dressed as a countrywoman and went towards the Dwarfs' cottage with a basket full of apples. She had cleverly poisoned one apple in the basket. The Queen knocked on the door and asked, "Dear, would you like to buy some apples?" Snow White looked out of the window and said, "I don't need apples."

"Dear, look how delicious these apples look! To assure you I will take a bite from one," said the Queen and she herself took a bite from an apple. Snow White could no longer resist the delicious looking apples. She asked for one. The Queen, cleverly gave the poisoned apple to Snow White.

No sooner had Snow White taken a bite of the apple, she fell down. The Queen was thrilled by her success and said, "Now, I am the fairest of them all." She returned to the castle, happy. Later that day, when the dwarfs returned, they found Snow White dead.

The Dwarfs loved Snow White so much that instead of burying her, they kept her inside a glass coffin. They decorated the glass coffin with beautiful flowers. The Dwarfs cried uncontrollably and didn't leave the glass coffin alone. They prayed and hoped for a miracle that would bring their dear Snow White back to life.

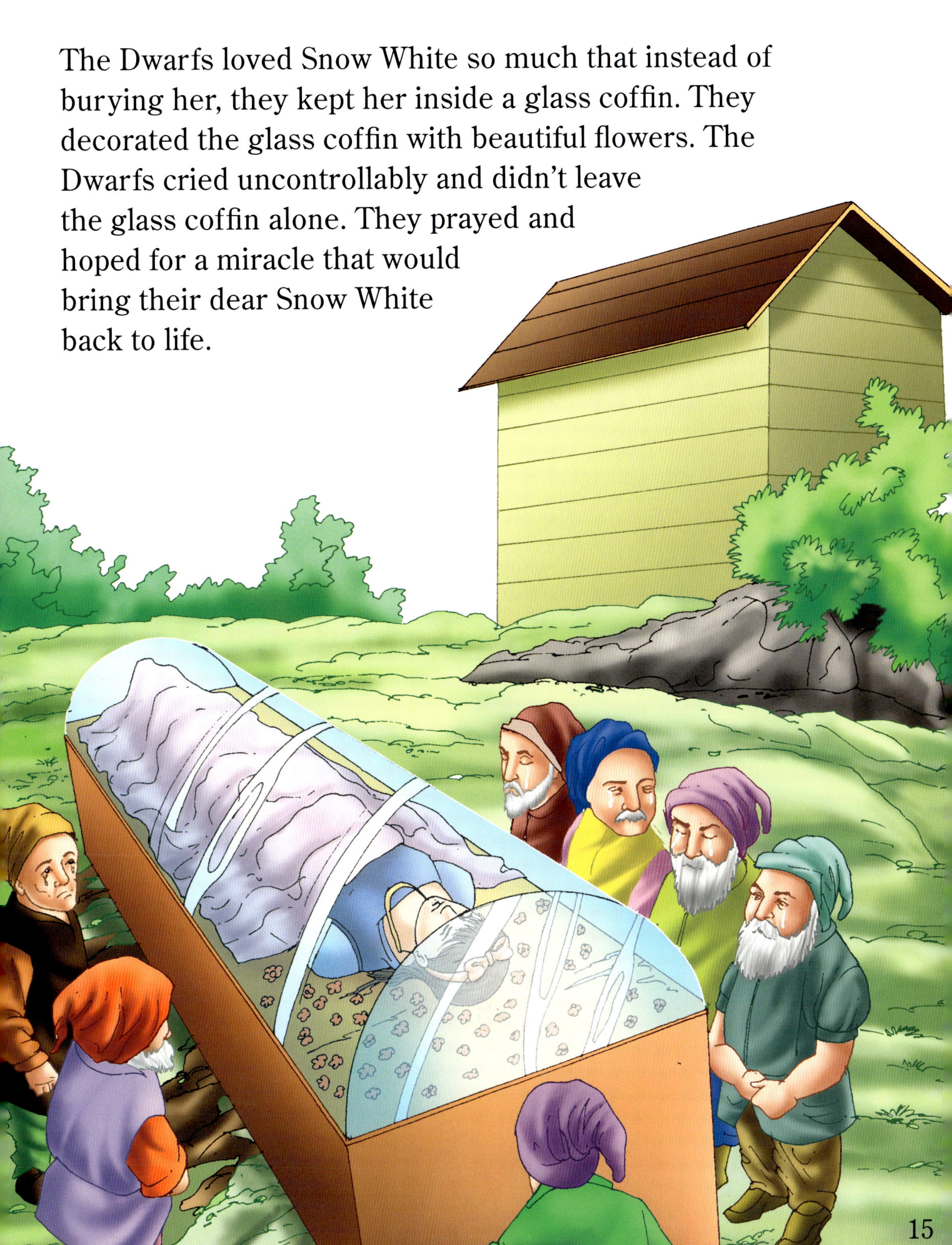

15

One day, a Prince passed by the Dwarfs' cottage and saw Snow White in her glass coffin. Instantly, he fell in love with her. He bent down and kissed the pretty girl's frozen brow. As it was a kiss of true love, Snow White stirred as if from a dream. She slowly got up.
The Prince married Snow White and they lived happily ever after.